The Sandman

Yes, there is a Nirvana;
it is in leading your sheep
to a green pasture, and in
putting your child to sleep,
and in writing the last line
of your poem.

—KAHLIL GIBRAN
Sand and Foam, 1926

Yes, indeed, there is a Nirvana;
it is in being the lucky guy who
gets to enjoy a wonderful trip to
Sandman's Land
every blesséd night of his life with
Barbara Taylor Floyd,
to whom this little book is
so happily dedicated.

—KEITH FLOYD
The Sandman, 1997

The Sandman

*A Little Book
with a Promise to Keep:
Rest, Relaxation,
and
a Good Night's Sleep*

KEITH FLOYD

Ten Speed Press
Berkeley, California

TEN SPEED PRESS
Post Office Box 7123
Berkeley, CA 94707

Distributed in Australia by E J Dwyer Pty. Ltd., in Canada by Publishers Group West, in New Zealand by Tandem Press, in South Africa by Real Books, in the United Kingdom and Europe by Airlift Books, and in Singapore and Malaysia by Berkeley Books.

Cover and interior design by Catherine Jacobes
Illustrations by Akiko Shurtleff

Library of Congress Cataloging-in-Publication Data
Floyd, Keith, 1939-
The sandman: a little book with a promise to keep: rest, relaxation, and a good night's sleep / Keith Floyd.
ISBN 0-89815-910-5 (cloth)
1. Sleep--Poetry. I. Title.
PR9199.3.F5644S26 1997
811'.54--dc21 96-45649
CIP

First printing, 1997
Printed in Singapore

1 2 3 4 5 6 7 8 9 10 — 00 99 98 97

Acknowledgments

The author wishes to acknowledge his indebtedness and deep appreciation first of all to Phil Wood, Ten Speed's Prime Mover behind *The Sandman*; to Kirsty Melville for her bright and insightful guiding light all the way to Sandman's Land; to Heather Garnos, for taking the book to heart and under her wing and seeing so creatively to the ten thousand details that an editor is heir to; and, finally, to Candace, who, having heard the writer read the story one morning long ago on *Canada* A.M., sent the most devastatingly charming fan letter one could ever hope to receive:

Dear Dator Keith

Thankyou For The Bedtime Story.
The Story Put me To Sleep Reall Fast.
I want To Give you A Gift But it is
Not Real. I' Amour l'Histoire Beaucoup

From Candace

Ah, dear Candace, wherever you are, doubtless now with little ones of your own, your gift is and ever shall be as real as real can be. J'amour ton esprit beaucoup.

Good night!
Is it time again to say
good night?

Is it time to pay a visit
to a most inviting place,
a place not far away—
how shall we say—
in inner space?

Yes indeed,
    if you please;
        and letting-go is all you need—
           to feel free as can be
              and perfectly at ease.
           Yes, now's the time for turning in
           and here is the perfect place to begin.

So, just relax,

    let yourself go,

        and have some fun in the

            sun-warmed sand,

                out—or in—

                    to Sandman's Land.

You see, strange as it may seem,
in is out,
and out is in—
as in a dream!
And all is well, as always, when
inside out turns outside in.
Then Sandman's Land's as near or far
as a blink of an eye
or a twinkling star.

4

But all this blinking and thinking
   is all it would take
      to keep even a sleepyhead wide awake.
         Yet let's suppose
      you let your thoughts settle down,
and your eyes stay closed.
Who knows?
   They might open wide inside, instead.

So close those eyelids,
  lightly but tight
    (if you know what I mean),
      and see if a sight
        that just seems to be seen
        could become a delightful dream
      with all the good things
    that sleepytime brings.

If you're as still as still can be,
  and keep right on breathing deeply
    in and out...
      out and in...
    there's little doubt you'll understand
all about this dreamy land.

In each deep breath is sleep that goes
to reach your fingertips and toes.
In and out…
out and in…
as every breath you breathe
goes deeper and deeper,
like magic
you'll be turned into a sleeper.

All set?

Let's set the scene for Sandman's Land.

Picture yourself all stretched out

in soft, white sand that's just so—

you know—

perfectly fine,

bright as moonlight,

warm as sunshine.

What a treat for your hands and feet,
shoveling down
and shuffling around
in this smooth and soothing sand!
And you may as well play along—
as long as you can.
Yet I'll bet you'll get sleepyeyed so fast,
the sights you see and sounds you hear
at last will fade and disappear,
till everything will make it plain,
this sand has sleep in every grain.

Now, as the sun sinks slowly out of sight,

leaving a golden glow in the evening light,

high up in the twilight sky,

crowds of billowy,

pillowy clouds drift by.

A calm breeze gently stirs the summer air.

Palm trees bend and sway, this way and that,

as playful shadows tease your hair.

You're really getting into this letting-go feeling;
going with the flow is so appealing.
Sky and sea and sun-kissed sand
all insist there's fun for everyone
in this peaceful, blissful land.
"Fall fast asleep," they whisper,
"fall fast asleep."
And falling fast asleep
feels so, so grand.

Before a moment more has passed,
     you're sure to understand
          all the rest in store for you
               in Sandman's hazy, lazy land.
                    Asleep? Or awake?
               By now, who can say?
          Such thoughts could make anyone
drowsy all day.
Or, what's more, it's quite all right
     if they make you snore all night.

But listen!

Coming this way:

"…chud'n-chud'n-chud'n-chud'n-chud'n…"

What's this hum-drum, droning sound you hear?

"…chud'n-chud'n, chud'n-chud'n…"

Sounds like a tractor may be near!

"…chud'n-chud'n-chud'n…"

Could be something fun to do.

Seems like a dream that's coming true!

"…chud'n, chud'n, chud'n…"

Hey, what could this be that's heading your way?
    There, see!
        In your mind's eye, plain as day;
    it's a yellow bulldozer not five inches high!
Though the dozer does look a lot like a toy,
    the fellow in the driver's seat
has a really neat job anyone would enjoy.
    As a matter of fact,
it's exactly the same as his favorite game!

He stops his dozer and drops to the sand;
and, with legs small as your fingers,
stands nearly as tall as your hand.
(Still, all in all, it's clearly seeming
someone here is merely dreaming.)
As you sleepily greet the little fellow, hello,
you feel the soft waves of a warm, inner glow.

Did you ever see such twinkly eyes,
  a smile as sunny and bright,
    or whiskers so downright funny?
     He's really quite a sight,
    all decked out in beachcomber's clothes;
  and out of his sandals poke ten tiny toes.
Add to that his sandy hair and handsome tan,
  and this can be none other than
    your old friend, Mister Sandman!
  (Or, if you're the sort,
call him "Sandy," for short.)

He welcomes you with a wink and a smile,
in his most relaxed and laid-back style;
and all the while, from hand to hand
his sand is shifting,
just the way we see time pass
in the sifting sand of an hourglass.

"Shhh...."

That hushing sound is made by sand
shushing, rushing from his hand.
As other sounds fade away,
you just can hear Sandman softly say,
"If you choose, I'll help you snooze
till tomorrow's dawn is up and gone."

You yawn and nod, so your choice is clear.

Shhh, listen!

What's this that you hear?

It's his tiptoeing footsteps close by your ear!

Those easygoing hands

and this sifting, shifting sand

let you know with a "hushhh" of a sound,

in a whispery way,

it's high time you let go to call it a day.

One touch of his sand, fine and dry,
lightly brushes each tight-shut eye.
As your eyelids grow heavy,
and you're all snug in your bed,
that warm, tingly glow is starting to spread
up past your eyebrows and over your head.

This sand just seems so pillowy-soft
and powdery-fine,
like moonbeams that shimmer and shine
without leaving a trace—
light as a fluffy, white cloud
floating about in soft blue space.

Feels like a merry-go-round is slowing down;
        and Sandman's fun has just begun.
He'll sprinkle his sand from the top of your head
        to the tips of your toes,
                though not, of course,
        where you breathe through your nose.
But first, here's some cotton;
        he'd almost forgotten
                to cotton your ears!

Now, like summer rain on a windowpane,
    the sounds all around
        sound so hushed and so deep,
    even night owls who don't give a hoot
for falling asleep may find they won't mind
    if they're happily napping the night away.

And in your breathing's ebb-and-flow,
    your breaths come and go
        like ocean waves whispering
            from far, far away.
        Softly whispering night and day,
    they invite drowsiness in—
and let sleepiness stay.

Breathing in,

    this drowsiness seeps way down deep,

spreading sleep throughout, deep within.

    Breathing out,

        like a breathy cloud on a wintry day,

           a little hint of a bit of fog

               hazily gathers overhead,

           then settles—lazily as feathers—

      down over your bed,

    to leave you sleeping—like a log.

In and out...

out and in...

it feels so pleasing to your skin.

Breathe even more deeply,

nice and easy, once or twice....

Inside and out; here and there,

the sleepiness is everywhere!

And now you really know without a doubt

what Sandman's Land is all about.

It's time to give up
　　to give in to his sleep,
　　　　for Sandman is up on his dozer
　　　　and down on his seat,
　　　　　　easing a huge scoop full of sand
　　　　　　slowly-but-surely up over your feet.

And the cushion of sand beneath your feet
    feels so comfy and cozy,
you're right if you think your foot on the right
    might almost be floating,
        it's feeling so light!

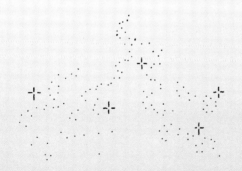

All over this foot his warm sand flows,

    trickling down between your toes;

        it overflows around both sides,

    then piles up high and hides your heel.

When it comes to feet,

    there's just no neater way to feel!

And the more his magical sand keeps piling,

    the more and more you're sleepily smiling.

With a quick shift of a lever,
  Sandman revs up the motor
and lifts up the loader to its highest height,
    with only a little bit more to sift and pour,
      until one foot's done
        and five of your toes
          are tucked in for the night.

Now you'll never have to wonder
how he'll put this foot right under!
Okay, it's safe to say
if your right foot is the one that's done,
it has to be your left
that's left undone.

So, back backs his dozer

    and starts in to doze

        by digging in deeper,

            right up to its nose;

        and that scoop goes so slowly,

    up over this foot and those leftover toes.

Though overly loaded,
     overflowingly so,
the dozer keeps going with all of its might.
     His sand is wonderfully special,
          all sparkly and bright;
               twinkling like starlight,
                    it's a marvelous sight.

As Sandman goes right on scooping,

more than just your toes are drooping.

It's all so real, it's loads of fun.

There goes!

You can feel both feet are done.

Say, you can tell it's really neat
the way your toes and feet just fell asleep.
And as the sleep-drenched sand
drifts deeper still,
the dozer shoves and fills,
and lifts and spills,
until loads two and three
have cozily covered one sleepy knee.

As carefully planned,
  push comes to shove again and again.
    Still, the sound you love most of all
      is when his sand from high above
    comes rushing down like a waterfall.

With four more heaping fills and spills—

as you just keep on keeping still—

both your legs,

you understand,

are all cuddled up

under a blanket of sand.

Time after time,

    the dozer comes and goes.

        As it hums and slows in a lower gear,

    the way to dreamland is free and clear;

        and, as always,

            you find yourself there—

              just being here.

"...chud'n-chud'n, chud'n-chud'n..."

    You're so totally relaxed

by the dozer's low and lumbering drone;

    it's such a soothing-sounding slumbering-tone.

"...chud'n-chud'n-chud'n..."

    This muffled, lulling humming murmurs,

        "Even deeper sleep is coming."

Seems you'll just never get enough
    of this dreamy, drowsy stuff.
        But Sandman's work is not yet done.
        It'll only take a little
      to sprinkle your fingers,
  one by one,
and make quite sure that none is missed.
    Again he creeps handily back on his tracks,
      and heaps sand on your hand—
        right up to your wrist.

Here comes a load almost too big
to be handled by such a tiny rig.
And when the dozer gets loaded
with all the sand it can hold,
you know it's time to let go
and let the sleepy times roll.

Shifting back to the right,
his scoop is lifting so fast;
but the sand goes sifting down
ever so slowly,
as Sandman takes it easy
and makes the moment last.

He'll dig one more big bucket

    to pour over this arm;

        and now, with a showering "rushhh...,"

      it's under a drift

        feeling cozy and warm!

Notice how everything seems to be slowing down
to the beat of the dozy
"chud-chud'ning" sound,
as Sandman swings around wide
and brings more deepening sleep
to your other side.
A wave of sand washes over this hand,
and its fingers and thumb also let go
to let sleepy time come.

Back and forth…

to and fro…

forth and back…

high and low….

His doll-sized dozer's slow, hushed creeping

means this arm, too, will soon be sleeping.

Ah, yes, it's true,

he's almost through,

for both your hands and your arms

are all snuggled up

under Sandman's charms.

Now how many scoops must he shovel,
    at best,
        to top up your tummy
            and the rest of your chest?
            Say he fills every scoop,
                and spills not a speck.
            Maybe ten,
                to spread his cover of sand
        on up to your neck?

We shall see.

　　One—hey, this is fun!

　　　　Two—like counting sheep to fall asleep.

Three, four—

bet you snore before he dumps four more!

　　Five, six—the old clock tocks and ticks.

　　　　Seven, eight—it's getting late.

　　　　　　Nine—

his blanket of sleep is feeling so fine.

And...ten.

　　You're all tucked in

　　　　right up to your chin.

A little here, a little there,
   a little twinkling in your hair;
and finally it's time for the finishing touch,
   so this must be the perfect place.
       Easy does it, not too much;
   just a blush of his dreamdust
for your sleepy face.
   Softly on your cheeks and chin it goes,
       and lightly trickles down your brow;
   then slightly tickles your lips and nose.
   Wow,
   it all seems like a dream, somehow!

Even your ears have given in
to the drowsiness, now.
And the dozy, drowsy sounds they hear
seem no louder than a dozen downy feathers
floating down, soft as snowflakes falling,
falling,
forever falling,
that never make a sound.

Another handful of sand
is all it will take,
until a marching band
couldn't keep you awake.
And now,
who can tell whether your sleepy head
is light as a feather,
or heavy as lead?

Well, Sandman knows
　　you're fast asleep from your head
　　　　to your toes.
　　　　　　So it's almost time for him to go;
　　　　　time, at last,
　　　　to turn out the light,
　　　and be drifting on—
　　right out of sight.

Before shifting his dozer

and easing away,

Sandman quite simply is pleased to say,

"Sleep tight tonight.

May your dreams be as bright

as the light of the moon."

But you can be sure
    he'll be seeing you soon,
        perhaps for a nap in the afternoon;
            or, no later than tomorrow night.
                You're the number-one pick
                for his next round of sand,
            and that's a first-class ticket
        to Sandman's Land.

Ahh, what could be better
than a good night's sleep?
What a beautiful way
to be all ready
for a brand-new day!

So away Sandman goes,

here and there,

near and far,

dozing off on his dozer

as it follows a star;

yet, sure as the sun rises and sets,

Sandman never, ever forgets

what a wonderful friend you are.

Good night.
It is time again to say
good night.

Z Z Z
z
z
z
z
z z z
z z
z